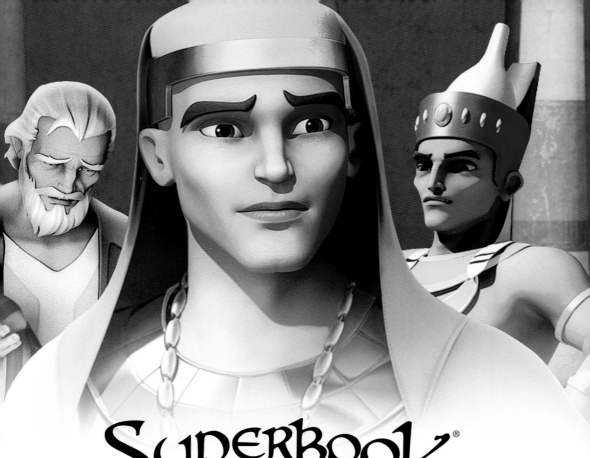

SUPERBOOK®

JOSEPH AND
PHARAOH'S DREAM

Most Charisma House Book Group products are available at special quantity discounts for bulk purchase for sales promotions, premiums, fund-raising, and educational needs. For details, call us at (407) 333-0600 or visit our website at charismahouse.com.

Story adapted by Jason Richards and published by Charisma House, 600 Rinehart Road, Lake Mary, Florida 32746

International Standard Book Number: 978-1-63641-012-8

21 22 23 24 25 — 987654321

Printed in China

Chris raced across his room and tossed some sports equipment in his closet while reading his schoolbook at the same time.

"Cleaning your room, forty-five seconds," noted his robot, Gizmo. "Reading your book, thirty-eight seconds."

"Yes! Right on schedule," Chris said.

Just then, their friend Joy dropped by. "Hi, guys. What's going on?" she asked.

Gizmo told her, "Chris has the perfect plan to complete all his daily tasks before we leave to watch the big game."

In the car, Chris explained, "We've got to follow my plan exactly, or we won't arrive in time to get the best seats at the game!"

That's just when Chris's dad, Professor Quantum, hit the brakes. "There's a car stranded by the road. I'm stopping to help."

"But Dad, this isn't in my plan!" Chris whined.

His father replied, "We should help those in need, Chris."

"Ugh!" sighed Chris. "I can't believe this is happening!"

While Professor Quantum was outside helping the other driver, a bright light filled the car.

"Superbook!" yelled Chris and Joy, while Gizmo mumbled frantically, "Changing our plans. Changing our plans!"

Superbook assured them, "I am taking you to meet a man who trusted in God's plan even though he had many difficulties."

Superbook set them down in a prison in ancient Egypt. "A prison!" complained Chris. "This can't be part of the plan."

Suddenly they heard a voice. "Who's there?" It was a man named Joseph. He explained that he was in charge of all the prisoners—even though he was a prisoner himself!

Joy asked, "How can that be?" So Joseph told them his story.

Joseph was from Canaan, a long way from Egypt. He was the eleventh of twelve brothers—and his father's favorite. His dad, Jacob, had made that clear by giving Joseph a colorful coat to wear.

Whenever his ten older brothers saw that beautiful coat, they were reminded that their father gave special treatment to Joseph, as well as their youngest brother, Benjamin. The older brothers did not like this at all.

While Joseph was growing up, God gave him some amazing dreams. Once, he dreamed that all of his family members

were bowing down to him.

When he told his older brothers, they became very angry. Joseph was already their father's favorite. Now they were supposed to bow down to him?

Those brothers were so jealous that they did a very wicked thing. First, they threw Joseph into a deep pit. Next, they sold him to some men, who took him to Egypt as a slave.

Then the brothers put animal blood on Joseph's colorful coat and told their father a terrible lie. They said a wild beast had killed him!

Joseph finished his story: "Then, while I was a slave here in Egypt, I was arrested for something I did not do. And so here I am in prison."

"That's so unfair!" Joy cried.

"I know!" Chris blurted out. "You need an A-number-one plan to get you out of this prison and back to your father."

That's when an Egyptian official came for Joseph. He looked very important and very serious. "Uh-oh!" thought the children.

But the official was Joseph's friend, and he brought news. Pharaoh had sent for Joseph to ask the meaning of a dream!

"The king of Egypt wants you to interpret his dream?"

Joy gasped. "You can do that?"

The friend explained that he used to be a prisoner with Joseph. When he'd had a strange dream, Joseph told him what it meant—and everything Joseph said came true! The man was freed from prison and now worked in the palace.

So Joseph got cleaned up, shaved, and went to Pharaoh. The king took a hard look at him and said, "I had a dream, and no one here can tell me what it means. I heard that you can."

"It is beyond my power to do this," Joseph replied. "But God can tell you what it means."

Then Pharaoh told Joseph his dream.

First, Pharaoh dreamed of seven healthy cows. Suddenly, seven starving cows came and—yuck!—ate them up! Then Pharaoh dreamed of seven healthy heads of grain that were swallowed by sickly and withered grain.

Joseph said, "God has revealed what He is about to do. For seven years, Egypt will have plenty of food. But for seven years after that, there will be a famine with not enough food. Unless you plan ahead and save crops from the years of plenty, Egypt will starve."

Pharaoh was so impressed that he asked, "Can we find anyone else like this man, so filled with the Spirit of God?" Then he made Joseph governor over all of Egypt!

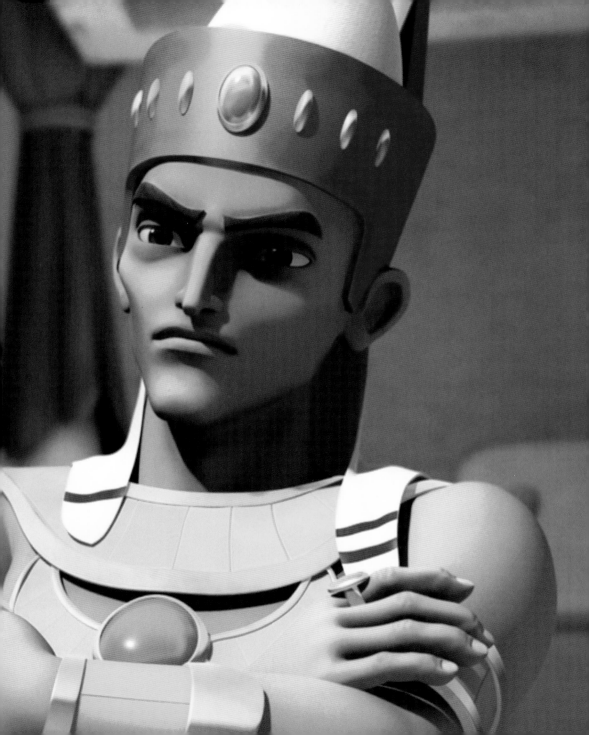

"Wow!" Chris remarked. "Joseph went from prisoner to governor in one second flat!" Just then, Superbook swept them away to the time of the food shortage.

There was Joseph, in charge of selling Egypt's grain to people from many places. And who came to buy grain this day? His ten older brothers! But they did not recognize him.

Joseph wanted to see if they had changed, so he tested them. He accused them of being spies and sent nine of them home to bring back their youngest brother, Benjamin. Joseph gave them plenty of grain for their family, but he kept their brother Simeon as a prisoner in Egypt until they returned.

Back in Canaan, their father, Jacob, was very upset. "Joseph is gone! Simeon is gone! And now you want to take Benjamin, too." At first, he would not let them take his youngest son to Egypt.

But when they ran out of grain again, Jacob had to change his mind. "Go back and buy us a little more food," he told them. "And may God Almighty give you mercy, so that Simeon can be released and Benjamin will return." So the brothers took Benjamin to Egypt.

There, Simeon was freed from prison and the eleven brothers bowed down before Joseph.

"Just like in Joseph's dream!" Joy stated.

"Just how God planned it," Chris added.

Joseph tested his brothers again. He pretended Benjamin had stolen his silver cup and said he would go to prison.

But one brother said, "Take me instead." That's how Joseph knew they had really changed. He began to weep as he told them who he was.

Joseph said, "All is forgiven. You meant to harm me, but God meant it all for good. He brought me here to save the lives of many people."

Joseph sent his brothers back to get their father. Then the whole family moved to Egypt, where Joseph took care of them.

In a flash, Superbook returned Chris, Joy, and Gizmo to the car. Professor Quantum had just finished helping the other driver.

Gizmo checked the time. "Chris, it is possible that we can still get good seats for the game!"

"Maybe your plan will work," added Joy.

Chris shook his head. "Forget my plan," he said with a smile. "I'm going to start trusting more in God's plan!"

"Trust in the Lord with all your heart; do not depend on your own understanding. Seek his will in all you do, and he will show you which path to take."

—Proverbs 3:5–6